MR MONKEY

PLAYS FOOTBALL

MR MONKEY

PLAYS FOOTBALL

Linda Chapman

Illustrated by Sam Hearn

Orion
Children's Books

ORION CHILDREN'S BOOKS

First published in Great Britain in 2016
by Hodder and Stoughton

1 3 5 7 9 10 8 6 4 2

Text © Linda Chapman, 2016
Illustrations © Sam Hearn, 2016

The moral rights of the author and illustrator have been asserted.

A CIP catalogue record for this book
is available from the British Library.

ISBN 978 1 4440 1554 6

Printed and bound in China

The paper and board used in this book are from
well-managed forests and other responsible sources.

MIX
Paper from
responsible sources
FSC® C104740

Orion Children's Books
An imprint of
Hachette Children's Group
Part of Hodder and Stoughton
Carmelite House
50 Victoria Embankment
London EC4Y 0DZ

An Hachette UK Company
www.hachette.co.uk

www.hachettechildrens.co.uk

To the staff and pupils at Wymeswold Primary School and to Jo Preston (the real Miss Preston) and her twins, Laila and Spencer. I hope you all enjoy Mr Monkey's adventures!

L.C.

Contents

Chapter One   11

Chapter Two   19

Chapter Three   27

Chapter Four   33

Chapter Five   39

Chapter Six   55

Chapter One

This is Mr Monkey.

He looks like any other cuddly toy. But Mr Monkey is magic – yes, magic!

Mr Monkey belongs to Class Two. His magic is secret, but one thing's for sure, exciting things always happen when the children take him home!

Class Two were sitting on the carpet. "Now, who should I choose this week?" said Miss Preston. "Jack, would you like to take Mr Monkey home with you and write his diary?"

"Yes, please!" said Jack.

Miss Preston smiled. "I imagine Mr Monkey will be playing football this week."

Jack grinned. Football was his favourite thing in the world.

"Mr Monkey can come to Football Club with me after school," Jack said. "Nick's picking the boys' team."

Nick was the school football coach. Jack really wanted to be on the team. Nick usually only picked children from Class Three and above, but Jack hoped that if he played really well, his name might be on the list.

"Please bring me luck,
Mr Monkey," he whispered.

Chapter Two

Mr Monkey sat on Jack's school bag, watching the football training.

"Good play, Jack!" The coach
blew his whistle. "Right, everyone.
Let's practise penalties."

One boy stood in the goal
while the others took it in turns
to kick the ball into the net. They
were all very good.

Jack waited nervously. He loved shooting goals when he was with friends, but whenever he was at Football Club, he always seemed to miss.

When it was his turn, his heart beat fast. If he didn't get it in, he was sure Nick wouldn't pick him for the team.

Jack ran at the ball and kicked it.

The ball landed straight in the goalkeeper's arms.

Jack trudged back to the line of boys.

Jack didn't score a goal next time either, and when Nick called out the list of the people on the team for the match against Woodbrook School the following afternoon, Jack's name wasn't on it.

Jack's mum was waiting for him afterwards. "You didn't make the team then?" she said, seeing his face.

Jack shook his head sadly.

"Never mind," his mum said. "I guess you're not quite big enough yet."

But Jack knew it wasn't
because he wasn't big enough –
he just wasn't good enough.
"Let's go home," he said.

Chapter Three

When Jack got home he took
Mr Monkey to his bedroom.

His football cards were on the
floor. He picked up the card with
his favourite player – Lee Tidy.
"I bet Lee was always picked for
his school team," Jack said.

He felt a tap on his shoulder.

"*Whaaa!*" Jack yelled.

Mr Monkey jumped up and down. "Sshh! If your mum comes in, I won't be able to help with your problem."

"My . . . my problem?" Jack said.

"You want to be picked for the football team," said Mr Monkey. "But you're not big enough – well, that's easy to fix with some **monkey magic!**"

Jack felt himself starting to get bigger . . . **and bigger** . . . **and bigger!**

"*Ow!*" he yelled, as his head bumped on the ceiling.

"Are you big enough now?" Mr Monkey called.

"Mr Monkey! I'm much too big! Help!" said Jack.

three

"What are you doing in there, Jack?" called Jack's mum.

Jack gasped as he saw the handle start to turn.

Chapter Four

Mr Monkey waved his tail. In the blink of an eye, Jack shrank back to his normal size, just as his mum walked in with a plate of jammy biscuits.

"You were making a lot of noise," she said.

"Sorry," said Jack.

Jack glanced at Mr Monkey. He was lying on the floor, like a normal stuffed toy.

His mum put down the plate and left.

Mr Monkey jumped to his feet. "OK, I think I got it wrong. You don't need to be bigger?"

Jack sighed. "No, Mum says that, but I know it's not the reason I don't get picked. It's because I'm no good at shooting goals at Football Club."

"Hmm. I think this is a problem that calls for jam!" Mr Monkey took a biscuit. "Jam is excellent for getting the brain working."

Mr Monkey and Jack munched their biscuits and Jack showed Mr Monkey his football cards. "This is Lee Tidy," he said. "He never misses goals. I wish he could show me what to do."

Mr Monkey leapt to his feet. "Bouncing bananas! That's it!"

"What?" Jack asked.

"Ah ha! You'll have to wait until midnight to find out about my marvellous **monkey-tastic** plan!" said Mr Monkey.

Chapter Five

Jack went to bed at his usual time, and the next thing he knew Mr Monkey was knocking on his forehead. "Wakey-wakey!"

Jack sat up in bed.
It was midnight!

Ten of his football cards were in the middle of his bedroom floor and his model plastic goal was in front of them. What was going on?

Mr Monkey waved his tail and he and Jack were suddenly dressed in football kits. They started to shrink. The football cards shimmered and turned into tiny versions of the actual players!

"Oh, wow!" Jack gasped.
Two of his favourite players
came over – Lee Tidy and
Dwayne White.

"Hi, Jack," said Lee. "We're here to help you learn how to shoot goals, no matter who's watching."

Dwayne nodded. "We thought we could show you some of our best goals and then you can have a go."

"Awesome!" gasped Jack.

"Do you remember the penalty I scored in the FA cup final last year?" Lee asked.

Jack nodded. It had been an incredible shot that had looked as if it was going to fly over the bar, but at the very last second it had curved down into the net.

"It was 2-2 and one minute to the final whistle," said Lee as the other footballers got into position so he could do the shot again. "I knew if I scored the goal we were going to win."

"I'd have been really nervous," said Jack.

"You've got to learn to forget everything apart from the goal," said Lee.

Lee looked at the net, his eyes locked on the goalie and he started to run. He kicked the ball and it flew straight into the top left corner of the net. Jack and Mr Monkey cheered.

"Now you try, Jack," said Lee. Jack glanced at all the famous players watching him.

"Don't think about anything apart from the ball," Lee said.

Jack took a breath. He could do this! He blocked everything out and ran. His foot met the ball and it flew through the air.

Yes!

It shot past the goalkeeper's left hand and thumped into the back of the net. Jack yelled in delight. He'd done it!

"That's the way, Jack! Try another!" said Lee.

Jack scored goal after goal, some of his kicks missed but most of them went in. In the end, he and Mr Monkey played five-a-side with the other players.

At last, it was time for Jack
to say goodbye and go back to
bed. "If you don't, you'll be as
snoozy as a dormouse tomorrow
morning," Mr Monkey said.

Jack thanked the players, then
Mr Monkey waved his tail and
the magic left the room.

"Oh, Mr Monkey I can't wait
until Football Club now!" said
Jack happily as he climbed into
bed. "Thank you for making all
that magic happen!"

Mr Monkey winked. "It's strange how Monkey Magic always seems to happen when I'm around!"

Chapter Six

Jack was running into school
the next day when Miss Preston
came out of the staffroom. "Jack!
I've just had Rajan's mum on the
phone. He's got a bad cold and
can't play in the football match
after school. Nick said to ask you
if you're free to play."

"Yes, I am!" said Jack. This was his big chance. Maybe he could finally show Nick how well he could play. He might even score a goal. He couldn't wait!

"Over here, Jack! Pass to me!"

"Come on, boys,
keep it moving!"

"Jack! Pass here.
Pass!"

Jack kicked the ball to Tom as he was coming up to the goal. Tom passed it back. The goal was in front of Jack with just the goalie protecting it.

Jack knew he could try and
shoot. He focused on the goal and
kicked the ball as hard as he could.

"Goal!" his team yelled.

Half an hour later Jack's team were two-nil up, and by the end of the game, the final score was three-nil and Jack had scored all of the goals! "Jack! Jack!" everyone chanted. It was the best day of Jack's life!

Miss Preston was standing by the door into the school. "It looks as if Mr Monkey's had a very exciting time with you, Jack," she said as Jack went to get changed.

Jack's eyes shone. "I'm the one who's had an exciting time, Miss."

Miss Preston smiled.
"Everyone always has an exciting
time when they look after Mr
Monkey!" she said.

Mr Monkey watched me play football. I scored three goals. Mr Monkey likes football. He does roly-polies with the ball.

I wish I could see that, Jack!